Ladybird Readers

# P ter Rabbit
# Goes to the Island

## Series Editor: Sorrel Pitts
## Text adapted by Coleen Degnan-Veness

LADYBIRD BOOKS

UK | USA | Canada | Ireland | Australia
India | New Zealand | South Africa

Ladybird Books is part of the Penguin Random House group of companies
whose addresses can be found at global.penguinrandomhouse.com.
www.penguin.co.uk    www.puffin.co.uk    www.ladybird.com

Penguin
Random House
UK

First published 2016
001
*Peter Rabbit* TV series imagery and text © Frederick Warne & Co. Ltd
& Silvergate PPL Ltd, 2013
Layout and design © Frederick Warne & Co. Ltd, 2014
The *Peter Rabbit* TV series is based on the works of Beatrix Potter.
Peter Rabbit™ & Beatrix Potter™ Frederick Warne & Co.
Frederick Warne & Co is the owner of all rights, copyrights and trademarks
in the Beatrix Potter character names and illustrations

The moral right of the author has been asserted

Printed in China

A CIP catalogue record for this book is available from the British Library

ISBN: 978-0-241-25415-8

# Ladybird Readers

# Peter Rabbit
# Goes to the Island

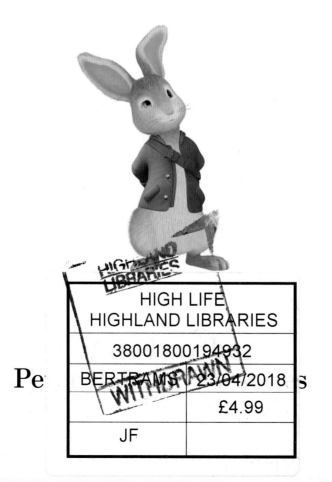

Pe                                    s

Peter Rabbit

Benjamin

Lily

book

nut

Old Brown

Squirrel Nutkin

raft

island

5

"Where's Dad's book?"
asks Peter Rabbit. "It's not
here. Old Brown has got it!"

Peter, Benjamin, and Lily run to the water.

"I can see Old Brown on the island," says Peter.

"Can we go to the island?" asks Benjamin.

"Yes! Come on my raft!" says Squirrel Nutkin.

The three friends go to the island. Peter sees Old Brown in his tree.

"Please give me the book," says Benjamin.

"I can help!" says Nutkin.

And he runs up the tree.

"Here it is!" says Nutkin.
"I've got the book!"

"He's got it!" says Peter.

Then, Old Brown sees Nutkin!

Peter goes up the tree.

"Give me the book!"
says Peter.

"You can't have Nutkin AND
the book," says Old Brown.

"Give me Nutkin!" says
Peter. "Let's go, Nutkin!"

But Nutkin runs into
the trees.

Peter, Benjamin, and Lily
run to the water.

"Here comes Nutkin,"
says Lily.

"Look! I've got the book!"
says Nutkin.

"Here's Old Brown again,"
says Peter. "He wants my
dad's book!"

"Here's a nut, Peter!"
says Benjamin.

The nut flies from
Peter's hand!

"OUCH, my head!" says
Old Brown.

"Let's go home!" says Peter.
"We have got Nutkin AND
we have got Dad's book!"

# Activities

The key below describes the skills practiced in each activity.

 Spelling and writing

 Reading

 Speaking

 Critical thinking

 Preparation for the Cambridge Young Learners Exams

**1** **Look and read.**

**Put a** ✓ **or a** ✗ **in the box.** 📖 ✿

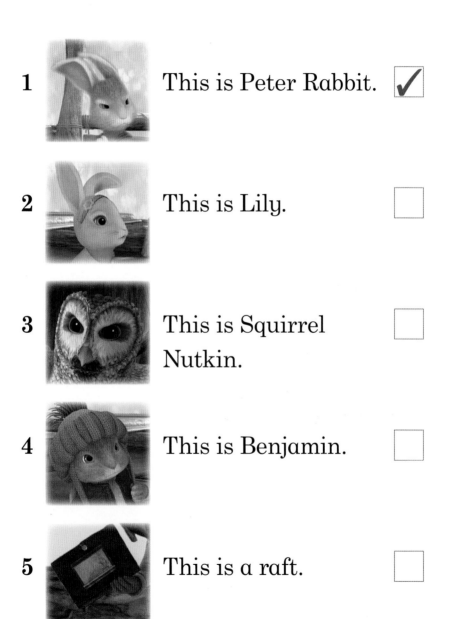

**1**    This is Peter Rabbit.    ✓

**2**    This is Lily.

**3**    This is Squirrel Nutkin.

**4**    This is Benjamin.

**5**    This is a raft.

**2** **Circle the correct sentence.**

**1**
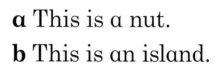 **a** This is a raft.
**b** This is a book.

**2**
**a** This is a nut.
**b** This is an island.

**3**
**a** Benjamin is wearing a black hat.
**b** Benjamin is wearing a green hat.

**4**
**a** Squirrel Nutkin is wearing blue trousers.
**b** Squirrel Nutkin is wearing a blue jacket.

**5**
**a** Lily's clothes are pink.
**b** Lily's clothes are purple.

**3** **Write *squirrel* or *rabbit*.** 📖 ✏️

**1** Peter is a ⎯⎯ rabbit ⎯⎯ .

**3** Nutkin is a ⎯⎯⎯⎯⎯⎯⎯⎯ .

**2** Lily is a ⎯⎯⎯⎯⎯⎯⎯⎯ .

**4** Benjamin is a ⎯⎯⎯⎯⎯⎯⎯⎯ .

**4** **Look at the pictures. Look at the letters. Write the words.** 📖 ✏️ ✿

ookb    tun    eter    ftar    lsiadn

1  b o o k

2   .........  .........  .........

3   .........  .........  .........  .........

4   .........  .........  .........  .........

5   .........  .........  .........  .........  .........

**5** Work with a friend. Look at the picture. Ask and answer *Where?* and *Who?* questions.

"Can we go to the island?" asks Benjamin.

"Yes! Come on my raft!" says Squirrel Nutkin.

**Example:**

Where is the raft?

The raft is on the water.

## 6 Do the crossword.

**Down**

**1** Old Brown lives on the . . .

**3** Squirrel Nutkin says,
"Come on my . . . !"

**5** Nutkin . . . up the tree.

**Across**

**2** Squirrels like eating . . .

**4** The three . . . go to the island.

**7** **Look at the pictures and read the questions. Write the answers.**

a

"Here it is!" says Nutkin.
"I've got the book!"

"He's got it!" says Peter.

Then, Old Brown sees Nutkin!

16

b

Peter goes up the tree.

"Give me the book!" says Peter.

"You can't have Nutkin AND the book," says Old Brown.

**1** Who goes to the island on the raft?

The _____three_____ friends.

**2** Who says, "He's got it!"?

_____

**3** Who sees Nutkin?

_____

**8** **Look and read. Write *on*, *next to*, *in front of*, or *in*.**

Peter goes up the tree.

"Give me the book!" says Peter.

"You can't have Nutkin AND the book," says Old Brown.

**1** Old Brown's foot is _____ on _____ the book.

**2** Peter is _____ Old Brown.

**3** Nutkin is _____ Old Brown.

**4** They are _____ Old Brown's tree.

**9** Ask and answer questions about the animals with a friend. 🗨

"Can we go to the island?" asks Benjamin.

"Yes! Come on my raft!" says Squirrel Nutkin.

**Example:**

Has Benjamin got a brown jacket?

Yes, he has got a brown jacket.

**10** **Read this. Choose a word from the box. Write the correct word next to numbers 1—5.** 📖 ✏️ ⬡

> happy   raft   runs   sees   tree

Peter, Benjamin, and Lily go to the island on Nutkin's [1] *raft* .

Peter sees Old Brown in his

[2] _____ . Old Brown is

not [3] _____ . Nutkin

[4] _____ up the tree.

"Here it is!" says Nutkin. "I've got the book!"

Then, Old Brown [5] _____

Nutkin.

**11** **Work with a friend. Look at the picture. Ask and answer *Who?* questions.**

**Example:**

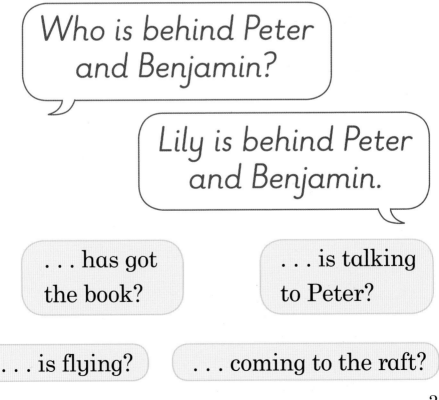

> Who is behind Peter and Benjamin?

> Lily is behind Peter and Benjamin.

. . . has got the book?

. . . is talking to Peter?

. . . is flying?

. . . coming to the raft?

**12** **Write the questions.**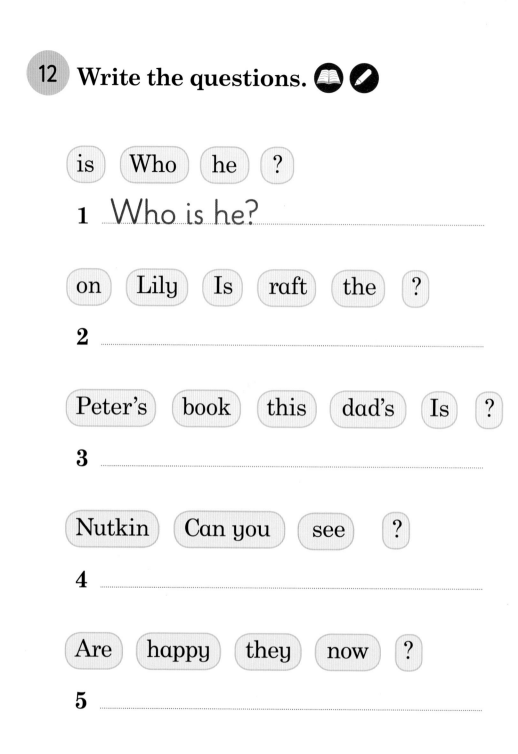

is　Who　he　?

**1** Who is he?

on　Lily　Is　raft　the　?

**2** .................................................................

Peter's　book　this　dad's　Is　?

**3** .................................................................

Nutkin　Can you　see　?

**4** .................................................................

Are　happy　they　now　?

**5** .................................................................

40

**13** **Circle the correct word.** 📖

**1** Who is behind Peter?

**a** Old Brown    **b** Nutkin

**2** What flies from Peter's hand?

**a** a nut      **b** the book

**3** Who says, "OUCH, my head!"?

**a** Peter      **b** Old Brown

**4** Who is not on the raft?

**a** Old Brown    **b** Nutkin

**5** Who is not happy?

**a** Lily      **b** Old Brown

**14** **Ask and answer the questions with a friend.**

"Let's go home!" says Peter. "We have got Nutkin AND we have got Dad's book!"

**1** Who is Peter talking to?

Peter is talking to Squirrel Nutkin.

**2** What thing have they got?

**3** Who has got the book?

**4** Who is Lily next to?

## 15 Order the story. Write 1—5. 📖

_____ Old Brown has got Peter's dad's book.

_____ The nut flies from Peter's hand.

_____ Nutkin finds the book.

___1___ Peter can't find Dad's book.

_____ The friends go to the island on Nutkin's raft.

**16** **Look at the picture. Write the answers.** 📖 ✏️

Peter, Benjamin, and Lily run to the water.

"Here comes Nutkin," says Lily.

"Look! I've got the book!" says Nutkin.

**1** Has Old Brown got three friends?

No, he has not got three friends.

**2** Has Peter Rabbit got a dad?

**3** Has Benjamin got a green bag?

**17** **Circle the correct picture.**

**1** Who likes nuts?

a

b

**2** Who runs up trees?

a

b

**3** Who lives in a tree on the island?

a     b

**4** Who has got the book?

a     b

**18** Talk to your teacher about the animals in the story.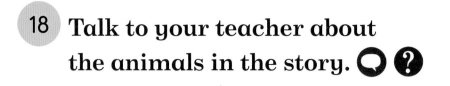

1

What do you know about rabbits?

They have got long ears.

2 What do you know about owls?

3 What do you know about squirrels?

4 What do you know about islands?

**19 Circle the correct name.**

a

The three friends go to the island. Peter sees Old Brown in his tree.

"Please give me the book," says Benjamin.

b

Peter goes up the tree.

"Give me the book!" says Peter.

"You can't have Nutkin AND the book," says Old Brown.

**1** "Please give me the book," says **Old Brown** / **Benjamin**.

**2** "I've got the book!" says **Old Brown** / **Nutkin**.

**3** "Give me the book!" says **Nutkin** / **Peter**.

**4** "You can't have Nutkin AND the book," says **Old Brown** / **Old Black**.

# Level 1

Ladybird Readers — Level 1 — Anansi Helps a Friend
978–0–241–25409–7 ☐

Ladybird Readers — Level 1 — Cinderella
978–0–241–25407–3 ☐

Ladybird Readers — Level 1 — The Enormous Turnip
978–0–241–25408–0 ☐

Ladybird Readers — Level 1 — On the Farm
978–0–241–25413–4 ☐

Ladybird Readers — Level 1 — Jon's Football Team
978–0–241–25411–0 ☐

Ladybird Readers — Level 1 — The Magic Porridge Pot
978–0–241–25406–6 ☐

Ladybird Readers — Level 1 — In the Garden
978–0–241–26220–7 ☐

Ladybird Readers — Level 1 — Fun with Old Things
978–0–241–26219–1 ☐

Ladybird Readers — Level 1 — Peter Rabbit Goes to the Island
978–0–241–25415–8 ☐

Ladybird Readers — Level 1 — Topsy and Tim Go to the Zoo
978–0–241–25414–1 ☐

## Now you're ready for Level 2!

**Notes**
CEFR levels are based on guidelines set out in the Council
of Europe's European Framework. Cambridge Young Learners
English (YLE) Exams give a reliable indication of a child's
progression in learning English.